For Molly

Clarion Books
a Houghton Mifflin Company imprint
215 Park Avenue South, New York, NY 10003

For information about permission to reproduce
selections from this book, write to Permissions,
Houghton Mifflin Company,
2 Park Street, Boston, MA 02108.

Printed in Italy

Library of Congress Cataloging-in-Publication Data
Denton, Kady MacDonald.
Janet's horses / by Kady MacDonald Denton.
p. cm.
Summary: Janet and her two small, well-behaved horses play
happily in her room until Janet tries to teach them new tricks.
ISBN 0-395-51601-3
[1. Play–Fiction.   2. Horses–Fiction.] I. Title.
PZ7.D436Jan   1991   90-33334
[E]—dc20   CIP
                          AC

10 9 8 7 6 5 4 3 2 1

Janet's Horses

Kady MacDonald Denton

Clarion Books
New York

When Mom was out, Janet liked to play horses in her room.

Angus and Anne were her two little horses.

Both horses liked to eat oats.

And to drink water.

Sometimes, Janet tucked her horses
into bed. They liked a good story.

Sometimes, Janet dressed up the little horses.

They didn't like that game.

"We want more oats," said Anne.

"We want to play in the meadow," said Angus.

So Janet fed the horses and led them to the meadow.

The meadow felt cool and the little horses lay down.

"Up you get," said Janet. "I want to teach you new tricks."

Up you get.

The two horses could dance very well ...

but jumping through a hoop was harder
and not so much fun.

"Enough!" said Angus.
"No more tricks!" said Anne.

The two horses shook their heads
and ran away.

Down the hill and into the field they ran. Soon they would be free! Soon they would be far away!

"Janet!" called Mom.
"Anne, Angus. I'm home."

"Have you had a nice time?"

"Yes," said Janet.
"My horses learned
lots of new tricks."

"Would the hungry little horses like something to eat?" asked Mom.

"Oh, yes," said Angus.

"Yes, please," said Anne.

Yes, please.

"Some oats and water?" said Mom.

"Oh, no!" said Anne.

"Not more oats!" said Angus.

"We'll have carrots and celery," said Janet. "I have two little rabbits who want to play outside!"